You DON'T Want a DRAGON!

Written by
Ame Dyckman

Illustrated by Liz Climo

LB

LITTLE, BROWN AND COMPANY

NEW YORK BOSTON

NOW you've done it!

I TOLD YOU not to wish for a dragon!

Did you already forget
what happened when you
wished for a unicorn?

The destruction?

The multiplication?

DING-
DING-
DING!

POOF!

POOF!

POOF!

POOF!

The **CUPCAKES**?!
Well, a dragon is **WORSE**.
MUCH worse. Trust me.

Just like with a unicorn,
having a dragon *seems* fun—
at first.

FINE! It's AWESOME too, okay?!

But once again, it's not worth it.
What you don't know is dragons . . .

and **DROOL,**

and what the stories
never mention is . . .

WHERE charcoal comes from.

Not to mention the **WAGGING**,

WHAP!

the **DIGGING,**

and the **SCOOTING.**

Dragons...

POINK!

BBQ CHIPS

I TOLD YOU!
WHY DIDN'T YOU TRUST ME?!

You just don't have
the space for a dragon.
In your heart, yes.
But in your house . . . no.

CORNER!

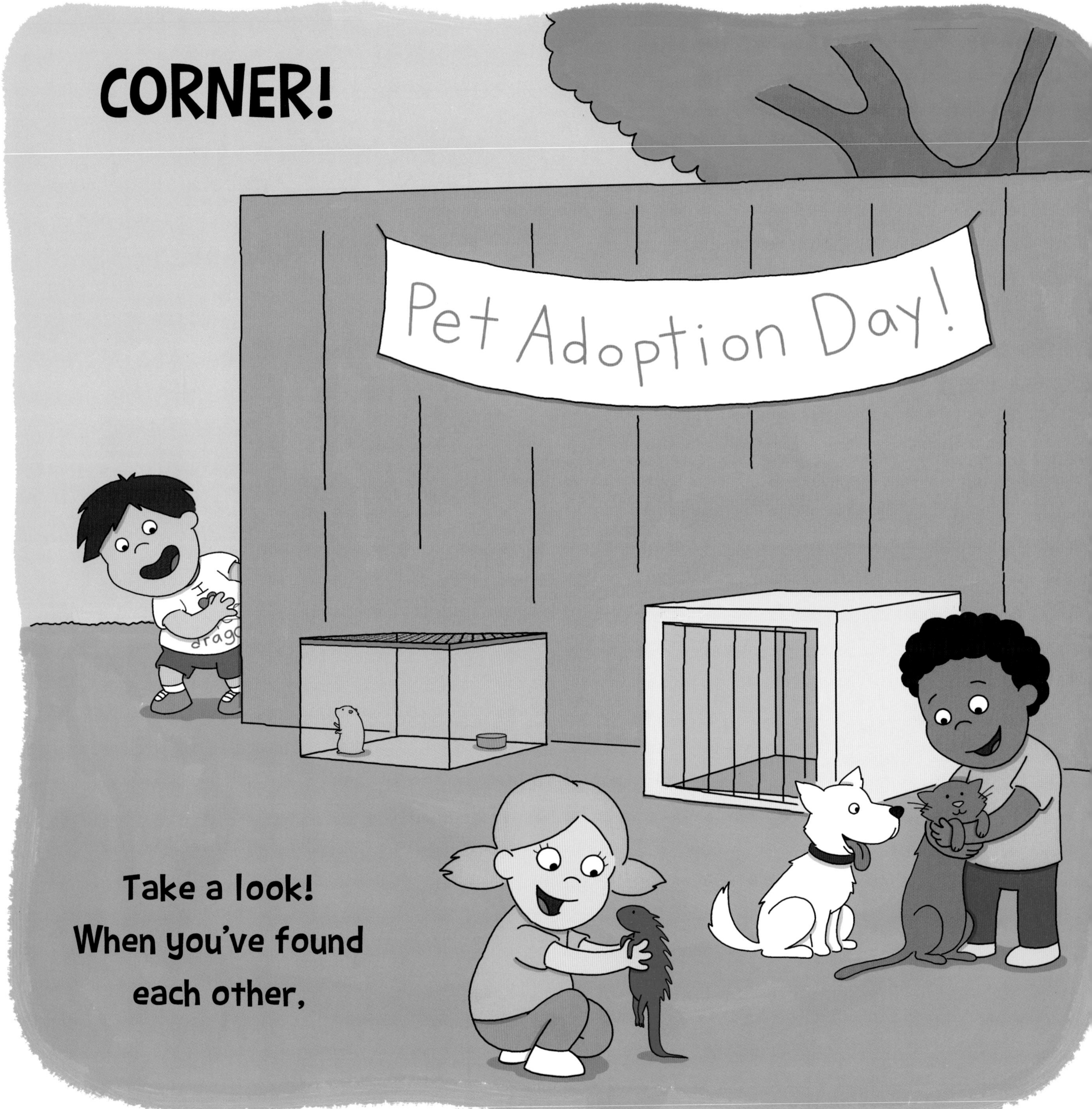

**Take a look!
When you've found
each other,**

you'll KNOW.

PERFECT.

Got everything you need?
Habitat? Supplies? Care sheet?

Good!

Your new pal can get settled
while you . . . tidy up.

WAIT! You **DID** put the lid on, right?

You don't want your little buddy getting lost. Or injured.

Or eating something
they shouldn't . . .

NOOOOO!
NOT THAT!
TRUST—

GOOD LUCK, KID!

To Mary-Kate, magical editor.
(You DO want a Mary-Kate. Trust me.) —AD

For Vida —LC

About This Book

The illustrations for this book were done with digital magic. This book was edited by Mary-Kate Gaudet and designed by Véronique Lefèvre Sweet. The production was supervised by Bernadette Flinn, and the production editor was Marisa Finkelstein. The text was set in Barthowheel, and the display type was hand-lettered by the illustrator.